Lola Bly

Lola Blyth started writing from a very early age. Being an only child she read extensively and also started writing with great imagination.

She was educated in Brighton and then for five years in London. She has now returned to Brighton where she is studying with the intention of gaining a degree at Sussex University.

Lola started writing this book at the age of 14 and completed it at her present age of 16. She completed the book and self published it on her own initiative.

She was awarded the School's Poet Laureate Award in 2017. Most of her holidays have been spent in Suffolk

January 2020

Lavender & Ink

Lola Blyth

Lavender & Ink

ISBN: 9781696396042

All material in this book is a work of fiction and
was created purely from the author's
imagination.

DEDICATION

To everyone kind enough to read my words.

CONTENTS

Caution   5

Wonder   39

Enchantment   55

Love   102

CAUTION

Strength

Native to fire,
she thought she
could lift his storms
all on her own.

Repression

We choose to repress some things.
We choose to repress the pain,
swallow the broken glass.
We choose to neglect the worst
things that need attention,
and we have a tendency to fear the
unknown

Door

They always said
that closing one door
opens another,
but sometimes the
doors get jammed

Angel

You placed a halo
around her head when
you first met her,
but it fell down,
and now it's choking
her

Lights

You can dance
around in the lights
all you want, but
sometimes the bulb
breaks,   and
your ego shatters.

Emotional

One of the best thing
you can do in life is put
emphasis on the good,
because dwelling on the
tragedies will only
make things ten times
worse.

Heartbreak

A map of your brain,
a transcript of your heart,
an over-wash of pain,
and a longing for a brand new start

Time

Held captive is time.
It watches a ribbon
that ties together
lives, minds and souls
grow old before its
time

Rush

There will always be
moments in your life
that throw out the
deadliest spin.

Floods and hurricanes
collide because loving
someone doesn't fill a
life.

Warning

You belonged to royalty,
and the crown was
dripping blood.

For a moment you served
out of loyalty,
but then you left open the
gates to your flash floods

Broken Record

An exquisite daisy
smitten with purity,
and made of grace,
only to become a
dandelion,
shifting and moving
with the seasons

Deceive

A chain of pearls was
your equivalence to a halo,
but little did I know,

silver holds the guilt of
gold

Royalty

You were honoured by so many,
but now you're only feared,
like a statue of the living
who was carved out of serving

Mysterious

You've got a
cloud of smoke
all around you,
choking everyone
around you,
and disguising
your smile as
mysticality

Status

You could summon the
whole world with the
click of your fingers.

But what would it cost
you?

How much would you
owe?

You could break my
heart million times,
and I still couldn't get
enough of you

Flame

Life was full
of aqua tones,
memories were
shaded,
almost as tough as
fire stones,
but we didn't let the
fire breathe

Karma

You built a tower on
false promises,
and now there's
nothing left to do to
break your fall

Let Go

Watching you
shatter,
you didn't show it,
but you've
switched your own
light out,
and now you're
burning out

Mutual

One man's fear
is another man's
delicacy.

And so,
we pay for each
other's crimes

Garden

Spirits in the
garden sing,
you were made
with no sense of
belonging.
A garden filled
with desire and
empty promises
that show no signs
of retire

Classy

What's your favourite
style of love?

Hers is breaking hearts.

Hush

She still thinks about him,
there and then.

His name is still whispered
across her mind.

But it is not silenced, and it
is not hushed.

Because she does not
believe that he ever let go.

You

You were once the
greatest person to ever
walk on my terrain,
the greatest person to
rule my kingdom.

But now all of that is
out of reach because
our souls became
poisoned by all the
time that we spent
together.
All saturated, dripping
in cool ash,
whispering a cold lust.

You made your
paradise from broken
jewels

Queen Of Hearts

Beware of the
Queen Of Hearts,
for she wears a
crown traced with
spite.

Beware of the
Queen Of Hearts,
she'll have your
head.

Two-Faced

The identity of love
stretches far beyond
infinity.

It tears apart souls,
and glues together half
broken hearts.

But beware.

Once you fall , it is
hard to get back up

Cold

Tainted words
slipped off her
tongue,
bright eyes.
Cold heart.
Waiting for her
love's demise

Liar

You can fake your feelings,
and hide them all under a glamour
that glows with a lustre
under the weight of lies,
but you're burning the truth into
existence

Unsatisfaction

During your lifetime,
people may call you the sun,
but keep in mind that the sun
can only light up half the world at
once

Contradiction

It's funny how
someone can burn
like fire,

and still be called
icy

Impact

I used to
constantly search,
always trying to
get to know you
more,
but now,
instead of
searching for your
personality,

I'm searching for
the darkness
behind your eyes

Simple

I'd thought
once that
tackling you
would be past
my depth,
but when I
jumped in,
I found myself
in very shallow
waters.

Forget

I was at one point
emotionally exploring,
and so I drowned
myself in all that
you had to offer, and
that's how I became
reckless

Lost

A wanderess,
in search of molten
pearls,
they said you were
danger,
set alight
by passion fruit
dreams
and red wine tears

WONDER

Beauty

What is beauty?
Is it art?
Is it life?
Or is it just what
we desire?

Love

Maybe the reason we're
all so hungry and act so
callous and cold is
because all we want is
to fall in love.
Maybe love is the one
emotion that we've
made a necessity,
and maybe,
the storm won't calm
until we have it

Darkness

Darkness is a phenomenon.
You feel comforted by its
companionship as you feel
it pull through your veins.
You feel scared and alone
as it pulls into your heart.

It's bittersweet and tragic.

Breathe

Her body is filled
with emotion she
can't quite define.
She searches
herself for answers,
but the search is
inconclusive.
The fire in her eyes
and her head is
calm.
Still on edge,
her eyes are bright.
Not with tears,
not with joy,
but with something
she can't quite
identify.

It feels as though
all of the oxygen in
the room was
switched out with
something heavy
and well disguised.

Butterfly Effect

Do you ever wonder,
what things would be like if the
universe had played a different
card?

Would you still be aching to hear
his name?
Would your heart still race at his
image?

Fascination

I am fascinated by you.
I am fascinated by the
way you move, the
works of your mind.
I am fascinated by your
speech, the way you
inject your language.
I'm fascinated by your
stature and by your
beauty. I find myself
staring into your eyes
with a warm, grounded
passion. Those eyes are
a watercolour painting
telling a thousand
stories . Silhouettes of
clouds and cities, and a
low burning fire

Petals

Petals
summon
your scent,
a wildflower
in disguise,
still uncertain
of your intent,
or of your
creation

Light

The light behind his
eyes studies me with a
satisfied admiration

Speak

When you call out to
something that isn't there,
everything still listens, but
is that fulfilling enough?

Wonder

Do I think
of you
the way
you think
of me?

Confess

Wavers of light
shatter from
your heart,
unsure of the
legacy you've
built yourself

Curiosity

You think the
sky is so pretty,
the way she
forms her clouds,
the way her stars
dance in her
night, her
eccentric
darkness
full of whirlpools
and chaos

Abstract

Words don't just
make stories,
they make art

Uncanny

His handheld glory
always wanted
engagement with
her carefully
balanced charms

History

Years ago,
feel their absence
deafened by
the force of living

ENCHANTMENT

Journey

Create your own story, a
fierce tale
of passion and love and
longing,
whatever you desire,
be the captain
of your own imagination

Youth

We danced through
our nights and
days, the lights
chasing us as we
ran,
young diamonds
using each other
to set our souls free

Power

Find your power of love,
to love all that you do,
and open it like Pandora's Box.

Stay true to your heart,
the most valued rulebook.

Believe anything is possible,
and be your own free spirit.

Drive

We're driving
together across
wide, open ended
roads

It's dusk and the
windows are
down,
to feel all that the
violet sky emits,
to soak up the
wash of pastel
colours,
to connect with
strangers along
the way,
and to get tangles
up in nostalgia.

Your eyes were
always full of
floods and energy
and character,
and your laugh
would always
enchant the echo
it would satellite.

Each time,
winding and
whirling its
way into the
air,

enough to
fill up
the saddest
of hearts

Travelers

We'd spend our
days drifting
eagerly through
cities and spinning
through landscapes,
skies and oceans

Poet

I may not be able to
perfectly understand
the world,
but I have my own
perception of it

Small Things

There are many
small things in life
that bleed joy,

like the number of
languages being
spoken on a plane,

or how sun rays
travel through a
person's hair,

and how a city
sparkles at night

Magic

Imagine a realm,
a kingdom of
spells and magic

where the
fountains ring
melodies
and the waterfalls
are a watercolour
page full of blues,
reds and violets.

Imagine a
kingdom full of
palace fairies who
dance under
umbrellas of
wisdom.

As you walk
through the
garden, be sure to
use only the light
of the moon to
guide you.

You must let the
sparrows fly past
you carrying a
fantastical
prophecy.

Do not fear
anything that you
meet ,
for it shall treat
you with elegance
and reassurance.

If you stumble
upon an orchard
full of apples
blushing with
content and
gratitude,
feel free
to go ahead and
take one for the
journey.

Let yourself believe
well and truly in the
kingdom, as it will
help your heart find
peace.

You must then keep
following the path
laid out by the roses
with soft thorns.

Listen to the
inhabitants sing
melodies of
enchantment,
humming along to the
whirr of the breeze.

Keep walking and
you will find

that the crown of your
accomplishments is
waiting for you.

Life Lesson

Remember in
your youth,
that young minds
can know best,
and that holding
wisdom does not
make you old
before you time.

Remember that
positivity is not a
form of
ignorance, and
that real people
can lead happy
lives.

Strong

No matter what
life does to you,
there is nothing
in the world
that could truly
brcak you,
because even if
you don't notice,
your energy
cannot be burned
away

Stars

You wedded yourself
to the stars
and the moon,
chasing them across
the broadwalk
like it was what you
were made for

Memories

Remember when
we were electric,
all lit up and ready
to sparkle?
Remember all the
picture book
memories
and the movie
scenes?

All of the animated
laughs and all of
the silent emotions
came to be the
words of our
classic story

Locket

I wore a solitaire
necklace
around my neck
and infinity
around my finger.
I wore a star
and drove to the
moon

Mind

You came to me
draped in crimson
and ice blue,
soon to reveal
all that your secrets
knew

Explore

I'm trying to reach
your intellect
before it collides
with your heart

Read

Flicking through
a novel,
reading into your
thoughts,
clambering up
all the mirrored
walls,
waiting for the fall

Grace

Let the grace of
heaven
fill you up,
cast your
self-truth
through a
thousand skies
and a thousand
new moons

Daydream

I'd love for you
to let me in,
to show me around
your thoughts
to tell me
all your truths
and all of your lies,
I'd love for you to be
my favourite pastime

Plunge

Let me take a dip
into your galaxy,
let me flourish
in all of your
colour,
let me breathe in
your dreams

Reminisce

Meet me
on the edge,
and we'll sit
with the sunset's
horizon

Drive II

Slip my skies
across yours,
slip my mind
across your
thoughts,
soft words
and flashing
road signs,
your energy is
burning,
and it can never
burn too bright

Dive

Let me dive in
deep into your
velvet oceans,
your heavenly soul
by my side

Space

They say that
once a star
has risen,
the only thing it
can do is
fall,
but stars are fire
and no one
can take away
that power

Red Balloon

I took the string
of your little red
balloon,
and it took me far,
far into space
through all of the
constellations,
and past the centre
of the moon

Spark

I can't be controlled,
rather,
sparkles and
shimmers of gold
ignite me
and help to set me
free

Ice

You're like ice gold,
cold to the touch,
but that touch
so replenishing

Selfless

Let her shine
and let her glow,
for each time
your love flows
to her,
she believes in
herself
a little more

Seaside

Dazzling colours
perfume Mother
Earth and by the fair
blue sea flowers
blossom,
perfect in form

Trust

Tiny pieces
one by one
awaken into
something magical
called
the faith of love

Battle

Conflict in
her own true place
exaggerated
self-unfolding, seeking
in truth upon intense
consciousness

Free

I want you to
remember
that your soul
is not bound
by any earthly
force,
not by anyone
else's existence
or capability,
but purely by
your own accord

Replenish

Turn and face
the wash of pastel
colours,
feel yourself sinking
softly into the breeze
that carries you
further than
you could
ever imagine

Individual

Part of this world
bears no relation to
the abilities
of your soul

Lanes

Garlands of
flowers down all
the sidelanes
blossoming
in exquisite
shades of violets,
blues and pinks

Chainless

Feel free
in this summer breeze,
let the waves crash,
thoughts tangled in
subdued cotton filters

Electric

She wore a mask,
soft velvet skies
all fell around her
whilst she ignited
all of her passions
in the electric
night

Escape

Driving south,
down to the coast, hair
loose,
sun rays
bouncing off our skin

Red Tape

We cannot change
the way we are,
but if we're happiest
living the way we
do, then nothing can
stop us

Hold On

Try to catch a wave,
running after the
summertime,
not ever wanting
to let go

Wordless

I long to write,
words firing up inside,
struggling to believe
that this is how we live

Home

I'm going back,
back to where
I used to dream of,
back to all of the towns
and all of the places
where the people shine

Adventure

Come on and tell me, what
do you want to know?
I'll share my life with you,
I'll take you to places
so high up
that no one else can reach

Translation

They say that
kindness is a
burden, that it
leaves you weak.
But it's a power
that got lost
in translation

LOVE

Touch

Feel each other's
touch
from a mile away,
liberty and
passion   raining
down on us,
moving in turn
with our energy,
mouth and brain
filled with
bittersweet
cravings for you

Castle

My castle clutched you
with steady hands,
sat on the royal blue throne,
your reputation
my holy land

Warmth

Your warmth feels
kind, like home to me.
You paint me with
ribbons
that caress my mind

Affection

I want to forever sip
your ignited flush,
your effervescence
and ever so gentle
touch

Cradle

I crave for your
hands to explore
my skin,
with a neon desire
for you to send
an electric rush
all over my body
to heal its ache

Delicate

Your heart is
wrapped
in white lace
and daisy chains,
as delicate as an
untied flower
bouquet

Home

His love for her
is an ambience.
He treated her
gently,
and kissed
her soul
for he knows
that she
is a home
and not
a temporary
shelter

Hands

My hands
gravitate
towards your
body, they journey
around your face,
tracing your
features
with a gentle touch

Broadcast

Your heart
is a light,
a satellite
that shoots
to the moon,
full of soul
and sky
and filled with
wildflowers

Happy

You are my sun
and I am your sky.
I am your stars
and your universe.

Together we help
to make the world
turn
and we help
the energy
to regenerate
itself.

Fierce

Burning bright
like a supernova,
make me hot
like a shooting asteroid
in the middle of
summer

Presence

Swing around
in a cosmic
haziness
your voice and
mine
so far apart

Brighton

I was feeling
lost and unsure
and so I came back
to the city
and things haven't
been the same since.

Raise Me Up

You set me free,
make me feel like
I'm on fire.
Our words have collided,
light up my night sky
because without you in it   my
stars don't shine as brightly

Calm

Stay where you are,
don't move too fast,
as I'll catch up to you
and help you breathe

Haze

Plunge me into soft
darkness,
you make me feel
like I'm living in
a state of nostalgia,
a permanent frenzy

Union

Everything you do,
the way you glow so brightly,
it's all a part of us

Care

He told me
catch a butterfly
and don't ever
let it go

Live

to help you
was a dream,
so much left unsaid,
but words just don't
come through
instead they start
a fire in you
deep inside,
a burning,
vigorous flame.
it gets washed out
by all of the colours
that you paint with,
and so I've learned
to let it all go
and to let you be.

Spark

you burn so brightly, the
brightest star I know,
and this is how
we ignite our love

Understand

I know I could've
done more,
but I cannot change
your ways,
or your mood that
swings to heavily

Dreamy

Dancing around
with you,
it's all an illusion,
but life with you
is so vivid
that I couldn't ask
for anything more

Passion Project

Sat by the window
in a dream-like
state
thinking about
other eras,
and pulling the
power of a
lifetime through
my veins

Connection

Drawing circles
on your back
whilst we laugh
about the pocket
sized things,
smiles echoing
across the room,
the light from them
bouncing off of each
other

Mood

I laugh,
merging between
the lines
of your
inconspicuous
nature
watching you
as you paint me
in all the colours
of infinity

Euphoria

take me by the hands,
golden in the night
we can do
whatcver you like,
dance together
in the city lights,
stay up until
we reach the sunrise

Printed in Poland
by Amazon Fulfillment
Poland Sp. z o.o., Wrocław

54501900R00078